The Big Secret

•The Good News Kids Learn about Gentleness•

The Good News Kids Series

Worms for Winston: The Good News Kids Learn about Love
Fire Truck Friends: The Good News Kids Learn about Joy
Aqua Kid Saves the Day: The Good News Kids Learn about Peace
Springtime Special: The Good News Kids Learn about Patience
One Big Family: The Good News Kids Learn about Kindness
The Trouble with Trevor: The Good News Kids Learn about Goodness
The Thanksgiving Parade: The Good News Kids Learn about Faithfulness
The Big Secret: The Good News Kids Learn about Gentleness
God Is Everywhere: The Good News Kids Learn about Self-Control

Scripture quotations are from the Revised Standard Version of the Bible, copyrighted 1946, 1952, © 1971, 1973. Used by permission.

Copyright © 1993 Concordia Publishing House
3558 S. Jefferson Avenue, St. Louis, MO 63118-3968
Manufactured in the United States of America

Library of Congress Cataloging-in-Publication Data

Mock, Dorothy K., 1941–
    The big secret: the Good News Kids learn about gentleness / Dorothy K. Mock; illustrated by Kathy Mitter.
    p.   cm..— (Good News Kids)
    Summary: The teacher at vacation Bible school uses a box that looks like a big present to help the Good News Kids learn the meaning of Jesus' teaching about love.
    ISBN 0-570-04744-7:
    [1. Kindness—Fiction. 2.Vacation schools, Christian—Fiction. III.Series: Mock, Dorothy K., 1941- Good News Kids.
PZ7.M7129Bi 1993
[E] - - dc20   93-6865

1   2   3   4   5   6   7   8   9   10   02   01   00   99   98   97   96   95   94   93

The Big Secret

•The Good News Kids Learn about Gentleness•

Dorothy K. Mock

Illustrated by Kathy Mitter

Publishing House
St. Louis

On Monday, the first day of vacation Bible school, the Good News Kids' teacher came into the classroom carrying a great big box. A pretty purple ribbon was attached to the top of the box. A big gift tag dangled down one side.

"Oh, good!" Harry hollered. "A present. And it isn't even my birthday!"

Teresa poked Harry. She said, "Silly! This box holds a secret, not a present."

"A *big* secret!" Winston said.

"Christmas morning I found a box like that under our Christmas tree," Amanda told Teresa. "My box had secrets too. It was filled with four *more* boxes."

Then Amanda said, "I just love boxes and presents and secrets. Don't you?"

And Brad thought, I hope this box is filled with presents. And I hope one of those presents is for me.

The teacher said, "There is a gift for everyone in this box. It is not a birthday present *or* a Christmas present. It is the gift God gave to us through His Son, Jesus. It is an Easter present."

"Easter?" everyone shouted.

Amanda frowned. She said, "I didn't know people got presents for Easter."

Harry was checking the box. He tiptoed around the box. He tapped each side of the box. He sniffed each side of the box.

"I know about Easter!" Harry told the teacher. "Easter is a time for colored eggs and chocolate bunnies and jelly-bean treats."

Harry took a deep bow. "That is the secret," he said. "That is the gift you will find in this box."

"That's dumb!" Teresa told everyone. "Easter happens in spring. Easter is over."

"I'm not dumb!" Harry hollered at Teresa. "You're dumb!"

Brad pretended to peek through a hole in the top of the box.
He yelled, "Yum! Yum!"

"Brad cheated!" Amanda shouted. "Brad knows the
secret!"

"Cheater! Cheater!" everyone sang.

"I do not . . ." Brad started to say he did not know the secret. He wanted to tell everybody it was too dark in the box to see. But the teacher held up her hand for quiet.

"Sh-h-h-h!" Teresa said.

"Sh-h-h-h! Sh-h-h-h! Sh-h-h-h!" everybody whispered to somebody else.

Then they all settled down to listen.

"I'm glad that you know so much about Easter," the teacher began. "But it hurts me to hear you call each other 'dumb' and tease too much."

"Yeah!" Brad said. "Treat me easy!"

"Exactly!" the teacher said. "When God made the world, He planned for people to treat each other easy. He knew that if people were gentle, life on earth would be happy."

"I try to do that," Teresa said.

"I try to do that too," Amanda said.

"Me too!" Harry hollered. "But it's hard!"

The teacher smiled. She said, "It is hard. We can't do it by ourselves. Even the very first people, Adam and Eve, had trouble helping each other. When they disobeyed God, they blamed each other, and they blamed the devil for tricking them."

The teacher taped a picture of glimmering light rays streaming from clouds in the sky to one side of the box. "But God still loved Adam and Eve. And God promised to send them a Savior. Someone who could take the punishment for the mean things they did. Someone who would give us a *new life* and show us how to live a gentle life."

"God sent Jesus," Teresa told the teacher. "We know about that."

"But how will we learn about the secret in this box?" Brad wanted to know.

Harry hollered. "First we have to remember all the stuff we know about God. Next we have to remember all the stuff we know about Easter. Then we can decide about the secret!"

Their teacher laughed. "You think about it and see what you come up with."

After snacks, Winston studied a book called *God's Greatest Gift*. Brad worked on a Baby Jesus puzzle. The words at the bottom of the puzzle said, "God sent Baby Jesus as our Christmas present."

Brad spent a long time remembering what he knew about God's gift of Baby Jesus and Christmas. Then he remembered what the teacher said about God's gift to us through His Son, and Easter. But what did Christmas and Easter have to do with each other? And what did "through His Son" mean? So he couldn't decide about the secret.

Teresa and Amanda were at the work table painting secret Easter pictures with lemon juice. Harry was at the work table too. He was making an Easter collage with glue and pictures cut from magazines.

"This is fun," Amanda told Teresa. She painted lemon juice lines in the shape of a tulip. She held it up to a light for Teresa to see.

Teresa was drawing an Easter basket. When she was almost through, Harry held up his collage.

"Oops!" Harry said. He bumped his bottle of glue. Glue spilled on Teresa's secret picture.

"You ruined my picture!" Teresa shouted.

"It was an accident!" Harry hollered. "I didn't mean to!"

Teresa was angry. She wouldn't listen to Harry. She snatched up her picture and tried to shake glue on Harry's collage.

"Be careful . . ." cried Amanda. Amanda wanted to tell Teresa to be careful not to spill the lemon juice. But the lemon juice spilled. It spilled all over the work table. It spilled all over Amanda's picture.

Teresa didn't know what to do. She didn't know what to say.

But Amanda knew. She gave Teresa a hug. She said, "You didn't mean to do it. That's okay."

"Let's clean up this mess," the teacher said. "You can make more pictures when we're through. While we're working we can talk about words like 'I'm sorry' and 'I forgive you.' We can talk about being gentle with one another."

Teresa and Amanda worked hard to help the teacher. Harry worked hard too.

It was almost time to go home when Brad said, "What about the secret? I want to learn about the gift in this box."

"You are learning," the teacher said. "You are learning by remembering what you know about God. You are learning by remembering what you know about Christmas and Easter."

"But when will we *know* the secret?" Winston moaned.

The teacher smiled. She said, "By the end of this week you should know about the gift God gives us. It's a gift that makes us very happy."

"I'm glad you're not angry," Teresa told Amanda on the way home. "I'm glad you knew I didn't mean to ruin your picture."

"Are you still angry with Harry?" Amanda asked.

I shouldn't be angry with Harry, Teresa thought. I'm sure Harry didn't mean to ruin my picture.

"No," Teresa said out loud. Then she turned around and shouted, "I'm sorry, Harry!"

And Harry shouted back, "I'm sorry too!"

On Tuesday, the teacher taped a picture of Baby Jesus to the box. The kids remembered all the things they knew about Jesus' birth. They made something the teacher called a manger-scene mobile.

Then the kids decorated eggs. The teacher said, "We decorate eggs on Easter and think of new baby animals because they remind us of *new life*."

The kids tasted marshmallow candies shaped like baby chicks, bunnies, ducklings, and lambs. But they still didn't know the secret in the box.

On Wednesday the teacher taped to the side of the box a picture of Jesus talking to children. The kids remembered all the things they knew about Jesus' life on earth. They remembered that He made sick people well, and gave food to hungry people, and told His helpers, "Let the children come to Me." They made a big picture about Jesus' life. The teacher called it a mural.

Then the teacher told them about days and nights and seasons—God's reminders of *new life* every day, she said. Then the kids marched in an Easter parade. But they still didn't know the secret.

They still didn't know on Thursday. They watched a video called *The Easter Story*. They walked through a maze that showed pictures of Baby Jesus in the manger, the things that Jesus did while He lived on earth, Jesus' dying on the cross, and Jesus rising again.

The kids made invitations inviting their families and friends to the Bible school closing program. They ate sugar cookies shaped like crosses. The teacher said the cookies would remind them of the *way* God gave them *new life*.

Brad said, "Day and night. Night and day. All I do is remember stuff about God. All I do is remember stuff about Easter. But I don't know the secret. I can't decide about the gift in the box."

"You *can* figure it out," said the teacher. "Just remember all the things that Jesus did. You'll soon know the secret. You'll soon know what the gift in the box is."

They might have figured it out on Friday, but that was the last day of Bible school, and there was a lot of work to be done before the closing program.

Everyone wanted to do something special to share what they learned at Bible school with their family and friends. It took a while, but they finally decided to do a play of Jesus' life. They spent the rest of the time choosing parts and practicing. No one hardly had any time at all to think about the secret in the box.

Almost everyone the kids knew came to the closing program. Teresa's brother Trevor was there, and their parents. And so were Mr. Milner, Mr. Knisley, and Ms. Meranda. The kids gathered on stage.

Teresa pointed to the picture of heaven on one side of the secret box and said, "God sent His Son from heaven to be our Savior, to give us *new life*."

Brad turned the box to show Baby Jesus.

"It happened one starry night," Brad said. "A baby named Jesus was born in a barn."

"His mother's name was Mary," Amanda said. "Joseph took care of Baby Jesus. But God was His father."

Winston wore a robe like Jesus wore when He grew up. "When Jesus grew up, He told people that He would give them *new life*— a happy life with Him forever in heaven. And a new, gentle life here on earth with Him. He showed people how to be kind."

Harry held his finger in the air and said, "No poking, please. And—careful when you tease."

"Jesus showed people how to be forgiving," Winston said.

"If someone hurts you or makes a mistake," Brad said, "you can say 'I forgive you and Jesus forgives you.' "

"And Jesus showed people how to love each other," Winston said.

Amanda and Teresa hugged each other and said, "Helping and hugging make you happy."

"Some people didn't like what Jesus said!" Harry shouted. "They killed Him on a cross and they buried Him in a cave. But that wasn't the end of Jesus! On the day we call Easter, he came out of the cave. He was *alive* again!"

"Only His life on earth was over," Teresa said. "He stayed with His friends a little longer. Then He went back to heaven to get our homes ready." Teresa sighed. "He did all of that for me. He did all of that for you."

Suddenly the Good News Kids knew the secret. They knew why Christmas and Easter go together. They knew the gift God gave through His Son. They knew how God gave them *new life*. It was a gentle feeling. A happy feeling. A "Hey! Listen to what I have to say" feeling.

"God sent Baby Jesus to earth on Christmas," Amanda said.

"So Jesus could grow up and die on the cross to pay for our sins," Brad said.

"And come alive again," Winston said, "so we can go to heaven."

"And have *new life* right now!" Harry hollered.

"You did it!" the teacher said. "You know the secret."

"Did we get it right?" the kids asked.

"Yes," said the teacher. She helped the kids open the box. It was filled with little boxes that looked exactly like the big box. The kids handed a little box to every person in the audience.

When everybody had a little box, the teacher helped Harry spread the big, empty box open to make a cross. "The cross reminds us of God's gift of *new life* through Jesus," she said. "And each of you has a little box that will make a cross. It will remind you of your new life, your joyful life, your gentle life."

And the Good News Kids hollered, "Hallelujah!"